Phebe A Holder

Voices from Lakeview

Phebe A Holder

Voices from Lakeview

ISBN/EAN: 9783337057169

Printed in Europe, USA, Canada, Australia, Japan

Cover: Foto ©Andreas Hilbeck / pixelio.de

More available books at **www.hansebooks.com**

VOICES FROM LAKEVIEW:

※ ※ ※

:: BY ::

PHEBE A. HOLDER,

CLASS OF '85.

※ ※ ※

" *The Assembly — a garden patch of the Millenium.*"
— DR. J. H. VINCENT.

" *Last child of the centuries, standing upon the threshold and facing the full blaze of electric light.*"

EVERETT, MASS.:
PRESS OF FRANK D. WOODBURY.
1897.

To the Beloved Class of '85,

with

The many Dear Friends I have gathered into my life at

Lakeview, to be "a joy forever," these "songs that

have gushed from my heart" are lovingly

DEDICATED.

VOICES FROM LAKEVIEW.

John H. Vincent.

"They that be wise shall shine as the brightness of the firmament, and they that turn many to righteousness as the stars forever and ever." Dan. 12: 3.

"The Interpreter then called for one Great Heart, and said, 'Take these and conduct them to the house called Beautiful.'"

"Now, the shepherds, seeing so great a train follow Mr. Great Heart, said unto him, 'Good sir, you have a goodly company here; pray where did you find all these?'"—*Bunyan's Pilgrim's Progress.*

Oh, Great Heart, pure and tender,
  Our leader grand and true,
We come with joy to greet thee
  At lovely, green Lakeview;
Thy presence, like the sunlight,
  Illumes the leafy grove,
Breathing a sense of comfort,
  A benison of love.

Thy kindly hand has opened
  Full many a long-closed door,
And left a shining pathway
  Where thou hast trod before;
An eager train and noble,
  A goodly company,
Follow thy leading footsteps
  To immortality.

The Master's hand hath crowned thee,
  His own sure signet set
Upon thy faithful service,
  Thy work for heaven meet ;
And when beyond the River
  We reach the shining shore,
The bells of heaven shall welcome
  Our Great Heart o'er and o'er.

On golden hinges turning
  The pearl gates open stand,
And full the heavenly chorus
  Shall come from angel band :
" Welcome, thou faithful servant,
  Thou blessed of the Lord,
Come in to share His glory,
  Receive His full reward."

Oh, what pure joy awaits thee
  In our Immanuel's Land,
Where souls by thee led upward
  Shall in His presence stand !
Stars in thy crown of glory,
  Shining with heavenly light
Forever and forever,
  With purest radiance bright.

Voices of the Framingham Bells.

INTERPRETED BY DR. VINCENT.

" Eternity, Righteousness, Charity."

List, afar the mellow chiming,
    Floating o'er the waters blue !
'Tis the sweet-voiced bells are calling
    To the grove of green Lakeview.
Lovely in its summer glory,
    With its shadowy, leafy dome,
Is the spacious forest temple
    Whither listening thousands come ;
Where is spread a banquet royal,
    For the eager, waiting throng,
Where the soul is thrilled, uplifted,
    By the power of sacred song.

Hallowed days and blessed teachings
    In this templed grove are given,
Seeming with their pure light shining
    Like an open door of heaven.
From our daily level lifted
    To this sacred Tabor height,
We behold a glorious future,
    Life is robed in purer light.

Oft as dawns each day in beauty,
  Oft as evening shadows fall,
Sound the bells in silver chorus
  With their triune mystic call ;
Voices **full of holy meaning** —
  Echoes from **eternity** —
Touch the chords of Righteousness,
  Wake sweet tones of Charity.

When the golden day is ended,
  All **its full, rich** lessons given,
And the tender benediction
  Falls like words of peace from heaven,
Through this grand cathedral pealing,
  Wake the three-voiced bells again,
Give response to holy teaching
  With a solemn, sweet Amen.

Laden with the grapes of Eshcol
  To our varied work we go,
With a loftier, earnest purpose,
  Well to serve, to learn, to do.
Still my spirit lists the voices
  Chiming ever peacefully,
Silver Bells of " Righteousness,"
  Charity, Eternity."

1881.

Prof. William F. Sherwin.

———

" He has moved a little nearer to the Master of all music."
— Longfellow.

———

Ended the songs of our singer,
 Broken the strings of his lute,
Silence o'er chords he has wakened,
 The voice of his melody mute.
Amid the pæans of Lakeview
 A minor key sadly must blend,
As we think of the chord that is silent,
 Which wakened at touch of our friend.

So freely he came with his offerings,
 His tribute of song for our dead,
And soothed our sad hearts in their sorrow
 As tears for our dear ones we shed;
And now we come with our tribute
 Of love on this fair summer day,
We keep in our hearts the sweet echoes
 Of songs he has left on our way.

Amid the green glory of summer
 We gather at Lakeview beloved,
Which seems all alive with his presence
 That 'mid the green arches has moved;
The fair grove of Lakeview seems waiting
 For one that comes not again,
The winds have a voice like a requiem,
 A sigh that whispers of pain.

We remember the bright, cheery spirit,
  The hand ever ready to aid,
The sunshine that came with his greeting,
  Now the **void** that his absence has made ;
We think of the home light so darkened,
  Now the strong father **love is withdrawn,**
The cheer of his coming departed,—
  The tender protector has gone.

Nearer the Master **of music,**
  The source of all melody **sweet,**
He has moved in loving devotion,
  The one dearest name to repeat ;
And the chorus of heaven has added
  Another glad voice to its throng,
To join in sweet hallelujahs
  The new enrapturing song.

" Worthy the Lamb,'' **they are** singing,
  The Master they love **and adore,**
We catch the refrain of the **anthem**
  And echo the **sweet chorus o'er ;**
And oft **as we're chanting the Gloria,**
  Our thoughts all hallowed **with love,**
Will recall the voice that has led **us**
  Now swelling the Gloria above.

When songs that we love are awakened,
  Old tunes familiar and sweet,
We'll remember the voice that is silent,
  Kindly the dear name repeat.

As we come in the dew of the morning,
　Where oft he has voiced our soul prayer,
Or **when in** the west " day is dying,"
　The vesper sweet floats on the air.

Bright are the fair flowers of summer,
　Sweet with their odorous bloom,
Rising from **out the** earth's darkness
　Like the Lord coming out of the tomb.
And so we take heart in our grieving,
　In the hush of the voice that we loved,
The sweet summer flowers have their mission,
　The smile of our Father, our God.

Lakeview, July, 1888.

––––––––

" 𝕴𝖓𝖛𝖎𝖓𝖈𝖎𝖇𝖑𝖊."

––––

" Press on, reaching after those things which are before."

––––

C. L. S. C. CLASS OF '85.

––––

The age is trembling with the steps
　Of our advancing Lord ;
Our pulses feel the thrill, and beat
　With sympathetic chord ;
The everlasting doors of Truth
　Stand open to our sight,
Along the shining way she leads
　We walk in purest light.

Her precious words inspire the soul ;
   Touch every hidden key ;
Sweep every chord with subtle power
   And wondrous sympathy ;
A large, **rich soul can always give,**
   Scatter its wealth around,
And, like the sun that **lights the world,**
   No poorer shall be found.

To meet the morning we go forth,
   Leaving behind the night,
And face the full, clear blaze, that glows
   With pure, electric light ;
Press on, while deeper meanings come
   Into the wondrous **years,**
And brighter, with God's changeless love,
   Immortal life appears.

Lift up your heads, O golden gates
   Of everlasting day !
Be lifted up! The morning breaks,
   The shadows flee **away!**
Strong 'neath the everlasting arms,
   " Invincible " we stand ;
" **Press on,** to reach the **things before,**"
   In our Immanuel's **land.**

" Press on, to reach the things before,"
   Our watchword still shall be,
Until is won the golden crown
   Of immortality.

From glory unto glory mounts
 The blessed path we tread;
"Press on, to reach the things before,"
 By God's sweet presence led.

July 30, 1885.

Gift of a New Day, with all its Possibilities.

DR. DUNNING in Morning Prayer Meeting, Lakeview, July 18, 1890.

The shades of night have passed away,
 The mists their light wings fold,
The glad New Day is rising clear,
 Radiant with rose and gold;
A new-born day with blessings stored,
 Waiting within the hours
That open as we onward go,
 Like perfumed breath of flowers.

The listening soul, throughout **the day,**
 Should keep **a waiting chair.**
That Opportunity may come
 And find a welcome there.
As we go on some spring flies back,
 Some door flies open wide,
Giving another trend to life,
 The Master still our guide.

We know that in the way we go
 He still has trod before;
We know that with His tender love
 He keeps the best in store;

So, reverently, expectantly,
  By morning's golden gate,
Before unopened chambers still,
  All trustingly we wait.

Watching and waiting but to know
  The sweet will of the Lord;
Then eager follow, as He calls,
  To do our Master's word,
And "hourly, as new mercies fall,"
  Shall "hourly thanks arise,"
As still His thought of love for us
  Comes with a sweet surprise.

Thank God, who giveth through the night,
  To His beloved, sleep,
And golden day to live anew,
  His own dear word to keep.
Upon this mount of privilege
  The bread of life we share;
So may we gather, that our lives
  Portions to others bear.

We will remember with each day
  The burden to be borne,
The sacred duty to perform,
  The lesson new to learn.
Thou Great High Priest, our loving Lord,
  In this sweet morning hour,
Thy benediction on us breathe;
  Endue us with Thy power.

A Sabbath Even-Song.

Fading now day's golden glory,
  Haste eve's deepening shadows on,
While sweet bells, for vespers chiming,
  Tell the Sabbath hours are done.
Day beloved, thy blessed service,
  In the temple of our God,
Brings us nearer, ever nearer,
  To our glorious risen Lord.

Hallowed hours we know together,
  Hours when heaven seems very near,
As we hear still, gentle breathings,
  Whispering that our God is here.
Hours of sweet and holy teaching
  Linger like a sacred charm,
Resting on the waiting spirit
  With a touch of heavenly calm.

Lift we now our hearts and voices
  In a grateful, earnest prayer
Unto Him whose love has led us
  With a Father's tender care.
Ever may the Sacred Presence
  Rest upon us from above,
And each varied earthly pathway
  Reach the home of perfect love.

Set to music by Prof. Charles E. Boyd.

John, the Beloved.

Read at the Banquet in Boston by Rev. O. S. Baketel, Founder's Day, Feb. 23, 1886. Also at the Hawthorne Circle of Pittsfield, Mass.

"There was leaning on **Jesus' bosom, one of His** disciples whom Jesus loved."

"O'er all the land **in town and** prairie
Are living forms that owe their beauty
And fitness to thy shaping hand."

—*J. G. Whittier.*

Hallowed and sweet among the names
Linked with the blessed Lord,
John, the Beloved, **has a** charm
Like a dear household word.
Hearing the gentle " **Follow Me,**"
All eagerly he came,
And where the Lord had set His foot,
He sought to tread the same.
And precious words of love He spake,
To cheer us on our way,
To help us in our work for God,
Till dawn of heavenly day.

Chosen from out the chosen Twelve,
To bear an honored name,
Nearest the one great heart of **Love,**
John, the Beloved, came.
The ages come—the ages pass—
The centuries circle on,
Until for us a child is born,
Our well-beloved John.
Like John of old, he leans his head
Upon the Master's breast,
And there he learns **the** tender words,
That give the weary **rest.**

And where he sees in all the way,
  The footprints of the Lord,
He covets there to set his step
  And follow at His word.
Like Him he labors " doing good,"
  Still seeking not his own ;
A ministry of love and joy
  Grander than kingly throne.
Chosen, anointed, taught of God,
  His blessed work to do,
To brighten life, enlarge its bounds,
  To make from old things, new.

Let blessings rest upon the year
  Enriched by such a birth,
An echo from the angel song,
  Goodwill and Peace to earth ;
A golden year that gave such boon—
  Our well-beloved John ;—
A golden light in winter set,
  A glorious risen sun ;
A cloud of incense shall ascend,
  With odors sweet to-day,
From myriad hearts uplift to heaven,
  For blessings on his way.

We thank Thee, Father, for the gift
  Of such a life to earth,
A life of loving ministry,
  That shows Thy glory forth.
Let silver bells of sweetest joy,
  Ring out his year of birth,
Let pæans rise from loving hearts

For manhood's sterling worth,
And sacred keep our " Founder's Day,"
   That brought such joy to earth,
We rally round our Leader grand,
   In growing numbers strong,
And bring to him from grateful hearts,
   Our loving, soulful song.

We gather round this festal board,
   Spread with Love's lavish hand,
And sit as at a sacrament,
   A heart-united band.
The lives that owe their joy and strength
   To thy kind shaping hand,
Thy name to-day with joy repeat,
   Throughout our smiling land.
From glory unto glory still,
   The Master lead thee on,
And heaven reward with starry crown,
   Our Well-Beloved **John**.

John B. Gough.

Read by Dr. Vincent at the Memorial Service held at Lakeview July 16, 1886.

" There was a man sent from God, whose name was John."

" Young man, make your **record** clean ! "—*Mr. Gough's last words.*

When last the Summer gladness came, his presence filled
    this grove,
His voice rang out in trumpet tones all eloquent with
    love ;
It lingers still, a sacred charm, within the woodland
    bowers,
Like tender psalm **with music heard in** memory hallowed
    hours.
The echoes of his glorious words, **inspiring in their** call,
Are sounding yet in **thrilling hearts,** like bugle notes
    they fall.

A mediator sent by God, with messages divine,
His life-work one with Christ the Lord, causing new light
    to shine.
To raise the fallen, cheer the faint, to bid the starving
    live,
Garments **of praise for robes** of sin, beauty for ashes give ;
Suffered **to feel the tempter's** power, to **sink** in depths of
    woe,
That he might feel his brother's needs, **his** depth of
    anguish know.

The Hand of loving kindness reached down through the
    darksome night,
And drew the precious soul-gem forth **to set in** heavenly
    light.

Angelic hand with coal of fire from off the **altar came,**

And touched his lips with power divine to speak as " In
His Name ; "

And crowned him lord **of glorious** thought **to stir the**
souls of men,

To lead great hosts **to victory by might of tongue and pen.**

O glorious **life!** O glorious death! fighting until **the**
close,

Falling with all his armor on facing the **deadly foes.**

We'll write in gold the last grand words, a watchword
pure to be,

To still lead on the souls he loved to immortality.

A true, strong soul, interpreter of **God's** eternal truth.

Though dead, **yet** speaking, living still with heaven's
immortal **youth.**

The aureole of silver light around the conqueror's brow.

Is **left** to earth, in heaven he wears **the golden glory** now :

Golden, because his life was grand, **a ministry** divine,

Golden, because its lustre pure shall **still forever shine.**

And Lakeview still **shall** honored be in Gough's undying
fame,

To us he left his matchless powers, the glory of his name.

'Tis **meet to** sing glad songs to-day, to drape his chair
with **flowers,**

For him who brought such songs and bloom into this
world of ours ;

No tears shall dim the summer day for the grand spirit
gone,

We'll catch the triumph of his joy, the victory he **has
won** ;

O **glorious hero !** victor crowned, what welcome **home**
awaits,

Abundant entrance from the Lord, within the pearly
gates.

And souls redeemed, **a mighty throng thy life and love have
blessed,**

With **welcome glad thy** coming wait **to** heavenly **love
and rest.**

Thy golden **crown** with stars is set, **the** lives to Jesus
given,

The **wandering sheep thy love sought out and led to Him**
in heaven.

Lift up your heads, O golden gates of everlasting day !

Be lifted up, a conqueror comes, open the **heavenly way !**

Vesper Hour at Hall on the Hill.

A Sabbath filled with love and **blessing,**
A Lakeview Sabbath, dream of heaven,
The Father kind to us has given.

As in the west " the day is dying,"
We gather in the hallowed Hall,
Where bright the **level sun** rays fall.

In this sweet hour with hearts all tender,
We listen to the heavenly word,
From lips we love so often heard.

As on the Mount of Holy Vision,
  We linger at this sacred hour,
  Feeling the blessed Spirit's power.

I sit beside my friends beloved,
  As one at our dear Master's feet,
  Hearing His word divinely sweet.

The notes of song in Sabbath vesper,
  Soft echo through the templed grove,
  Like voice of angel choir above.

And now in holy benediction,
  Is breathed the sweetest, tender prayer,
  That God would keep us in His care.

Go with us all through varied pathway,
  Until the day of life shall wane,
  " God with us till we meet again."

Still doth the holy memory linger—
  The vesper hour—so sweet, God-given,
  With light that shone o'er us from heaven.

At Lakeview Assembly, Aug. 4, 1895.

A Morning Hour in Idlewood.

Dedicated to the Beloved Idlewood Ten.

Golden fell the morning sunshine
  On the grove at loved Lakeview,
  While the peace of heaven seemed brooding
  In the dome of melting blue;

Idlewood, with shades inviting,
Lured us by a mystic charm;
'Mid green leaves the low winds whispered,
Sweet the air with breath of balm.

Gathered here **a group of** maidens,
As the morning, **fair and sweet;**
Coming with warm hearts love laden,
Listening sat at Wisdom's feet.
Listening, while the bright, young faces
Shone with inspiration given,
As one who had learned of Jesus
Gave his message, words from heaven.

Message from the blessed Master,
From His life the golden **word,**
"In His Name" to live and labor,
Blessing others, doing good;
And a sacred, unseen presence
Filled with love the morning hour,
Idlewood **became a Bethel,**
Hallowed place, the leafy **bower.**

One was there **whose face** was lighted
With the **love and** peace of heaven—
Marion, our sweet young **sister,**
Whose bright **life** is freely given
Unto Him whose steps she **follows—**
Jesus, her beloved Lord,
Bearing far, to lives in darkness,
Blessings from His glorious Word.

E'en as if a door in heaven
   Had been opened for us there,
Seemed that hour of love and worship,
   Full of joy unearthly fair;
From the wildwood **altar rising**,
   Incense came with **odors** sweet,
Prayer from loving hearts united,
   Rising to the Mercy Seat

For a blessing on our sister,
   For the Lord to go before,
Leading her with **loving kindness**,
   Where He opens wide the door.
Still the very light of heaven
   Rested on the fair young face,
The sweet **spirit of** the Master,
   His own benison **of** peace.

Oft will rise a memory tender
   Of that woodland scene so fair;
Pictures of love-lighted faces,
   Of the brown head bowed **in prayer**;
And the memory long shall linger,
   Like a mother-hallowed psalm,
Coming still when cares are pressing,
   With a touch of heavenly calm.

Marion! when the Orient echoes
   Wake with Moslem call to prayer,
Let this hour so blessed waken, .
   See again this picture fair;

Think of all the treasures gathered,
　　Hallowed days of dear Lakeview;
　　Precious friends whose hearts will ever
　　Beat with love and prayer for you.

July 23, 1886.

An Evening Hour in Idlewood.

FIVE YEARS LATER.

Closed the sweet hour of vesper service,
　　Hushed voices of the waiting throng
　　Blending as one in holy **song**.

The sunset gold lights up with glory
　　The cloudbed **of the dying day,**
　　Passing with lingering grace away.

Down from the mount of hallowed vision
　　I seek a peopled solitude,
　　The charméd shades of Idlewood.

I mind me of **a** radiant morning,
　　A lustrum full of years has gone,
　　Since that love-lighted, wondrous dawn.

When 'neath these woodland shades there gathered
　　To bow before the Father's throne,
　　The Sister Ten, **in** love made one.

Here is our shrine, our spirit altar,
　　And here still glows the sacred flame,
　　" For love of Christ," and " In His Name."

Alone I sit beneath the shadows,
And each beloved name I call,
Praying the Father bless them all.

I see the group in vision tender,
The dear young sister faces sweet,
Who listening sat at Wisdom's feet.

Where are the nine? I'm left, I only,
To seek the Mecca of our love,
And constant at the altar prove.

Yet not in Idlewood beloved
The faithful Ten may now be found,
Apart we serve on hallowed ground.

All one in heart, O blessed Father,
Our spirits blend in love to Thee,
Though severed wide by mount and sea.

IDLEWOOD, July, 1891.

Ten Years After.

1886.   July 23.   1896.

IDLEWOOD TEN.

"How comforting the thought expressed by Mrs. Davis in her prayer that never-to-be-forgotten morning : 'We may never meet again here, but one day we shall meet, and on the banks of the River that flows by the Great White Throne we may sit down and talk it all over together.'"

—*Letter from Dora M. Wing, one of the Idlewood Ten.*

Through the years our thoughts are turning
To that golden lighted morn,
When in Idlewood we gathered,
In the dewy, sparkling dawn.

When that band of loving daughters
　Brought their glad heart-offering,
Gave themselves anew in service,
　Unto Christ, their Lord and King,
　　　　Ten years ago.

Nevermore on this side heaven,
　May our band united be,
Nevermore as then to mingle
　Looks and tones of sympathy.
Forth unto our work for others,
　We have gone still one in heart.
Glad in any loving service
　With our Lord to have a part,
　　　　As Ten Years ago.

" In His Name " upon our banner,
　We have loved the precious word,
Loved to follow in the footsteps
　Of the Christ, our Master, Lord.
May His spirit ever with us
　From our lives in beauty shine,
Changed from glory unto glory
　By His power of love divine.

And one day—one day, most blessed,
　When the life of earth is o'er,
We shall meet " Beyond the River,"
　There to dwell forevermore.
On the banks of that fair River,
　Flowing by the Great White Throne,
We shall come by varied pathways,
　We shall gather one by one.

By that crystal flowing River,
  Under arching Tree of Life,
We may sit and talk all over
  Days with dear earth memories rife.
Severed lives, yet one in spirit,
  With our gathered sheaves we **come**,
North and South, East, West gates bringing
  All to the dear Father's home.

Ten glad years in Thy earth vineyard,
  Thou hast spared **us all** to live,
And again, dear Lord and Master,
  Unto Thee, ourselves we give.
Scattered all—one band united,
  Loving Thee yet more and more,
With one heart may we press onward,
  Reaching after things before.

Then in **heaven's long, sweet** communion,
  There'll be time enough to say
All our hearts have **kept long** silent,
  Through the parted **earthly way.**
Oh how blessed! Home forever!
  We have come, we're here to stay,
For the King His daughters welcomes,
  Here to love and serve alway

I Had a Friend.

"Thine they were, and thou gavest them me."

"**The beauty of** Friendship is its infinity."—*Professor Drummond.*

"It is so good to have a friend in the world."

—*Mrs. A. D. T. Whitney.*

When first I met I knew my friend
 By soul of answering sympathy ;
The holy harmony within,
 Thy gentle presence brought **to me.**
O gift of God, my precious friend,
 Thou wert His own, He gave to me
Rare treasure to enrich my life
 From out His own infinity.

The dear Lord sets His heavenly seal
 Upon the face of holy friend,
And in the features that we love
 The human and divine oft blend.
Some natures in their love for us
 Inspire us with **their own pure love,**
To consecrate our **lives anew,**
 To make us fit for life above.

My friend, the brightener of my life,
 To double joys, all griefs divide,
A counsellor, a strengthener still,
 Uplifter, faithful, at my side.
True friends are nearest unto God
 When nearest each to other's heart ;
When thought and love in Him unite,
 The holy bond death cannot part.

O treasured friend !   O rarest boon,
  That came to me in Lakeview Grove,
This sacred joy to crown my life,
  From God's own hand the gift of love.
Thy presence elevates, inspires,
  The finest chords it lingers o'**er**,
Wakens a music in my soul
  That I knew not was there before.

I feel thy soul in stillness sweet,
  The thought, responsive, answering mine,
I need not voice, or words from thee,
  I've learned thy language to divine.
Love's benediction let me breathe,
  In this our Sabbath vesper hour,
Our dear Lord's sweetest gifts be thine,
  His presence be life's richest dower.

His peace, His blessed peace be thine,
  His gladness in thy heart abide,
His presence consecrate thy life,
  His light thy footsteps ever **guide**.
O;life and love !   O memory dear
  With friendship's sweet infinity !
I lift again our Poet's prayer,
  '' Each possible good wish for thee.''

"Miss Holder's Flossie."

TEN YEARS.

Brightly the soft skies of summer
  Were arching the grove at Lakeview,
The green trees waved their leaf branches
  As the rays of gold-light shone through
Amid the scenes all so love-hallowed
  There came on that rare summer day
A joyous surprise, sweet and tender,
  That still gladdens my life with its ray,
      Ten years ago.

Before me uprose a sweet presence,
  Like wood-nymph or graceful robed sprite,
With smiles and soft voice of greeting,
  A vision of love and delight.
How plainly I see the fair picture,
  How bright the memory appears,
As I look through the rainbow-hued arches,
  The vista of ten loving years —
      Ten years ago.

My Flossie, a joy and a blessing,
  Enriching my life with her love,
Still into my heart closer nestling,
  As swiftly the circling years move.
Anew I thank the dear Father,
  As I think of the sweet summer day,
For the rare wealth of love, true and tender,
  That gladdened my life with its ray
      Ten years ago.

And now as the decade is rounded
  As we stand on this height, 'mid the years,
We look back to trace the life pathway
  All bright with true love it appears.
In my heart a sweet benediction
  Is rising and singing to-day,
That God's peace and love rich with blessing
  May abide with my darling alway.
                God's peace with my Flossie alway

July 25, 1884-1894.

Ἀθε Sabbath Vesper Hour.

Set to music by Prof. WILLIAM F. GIBSON, New Hampshire Conference Seminary, Tilton, N. H.

In my heart a song is rising
  Holy peace of twilight psalm,
As the Sabbath breathes its blessing,
  Vesper **hour of hallowed** calm.
Thought **of God among us** fallen,
  Kindled **by** His breath divine,
Is the wondrous power uniting
  Myriad **hearts at vesper shrine.**

Vesper hour—the soul at leisure
  Climbs a sacred Pisgah height,
Views the Promised Land before us,
  Arched by God's bright bow of light;
Earth and heaven seem meeting, blending,
  In this richly freighted hour,
Wondrous is the presence round us,
  Thrilling with **a** mystic power.

Clouds of incense sweet ascending
  From heart altars to the Lord,
Prayers from loving, waiting servants,
  One before the throne of **God.**
Added sweetness to the Sabbath
  Comes with vesper hallowed time,
Like sweet bells in silver chorus,
  With their mellow, distant chime.

Some glad day, 'neath flowery arches
  Of our Heavenly Father's love,
Through the gates into the City
  May we pass **to joy** above ;
When this hour that seems the portal
  Of the home unseen that waits,
Shall lead up to light immortal,
  Just beyond the pearly gates.
Here we list the sweet-toned echo,
  In our Father's gracious **word,**
There we join the sounding anthem,
  "Alleluia ! Praise the Lord !"

1890.

Four Girls at Lakeview.

A la Pansy.

The **summer** calls with voice of joy,
  The winds are soft, blue skies are bright,
The air like balm with odorous bloom,
  The green earth floats in amber light.

A voice is in the vibrant air,
  Our waiting hearts know well the call,
Sweet bells of Lakeview wake again,
  The mellow chimes in music fall.

We hasten to our hallowed grove,
  Our friends beloved again to greet;
With hearts aglow, with spirits light,
  Four girls at Lakeview joyful meet.
Our Flossie with her gentle grace,
  Carrie, with loving heart and true,
Dora, with presence full of joy,
  While Phebe sings her song for you.

A charmed quartette, with hearts as one,
  We live within this blessed place
As in a chamber close to heaven,
  Where God reveals His smiling face.
We linger 'neath the whispering trees,
  With eager steps we climb the hill,
We list to Wisdom's golden words—
  Pure gold—our hearts with love to fill.

Our lovely grove, with pillared shade,
  High overarched with summer green,
Where perfumed zephyrs softly play,
  And echoing walks are found between;
A clear, ideal atmosphere,
  From out whose depths rich blessings fall,
Descending like life-giving dews,
  A magic power, uplifting all.

We gather in loved Normal Hall,
  Beneath the morning's golden ray,
Where Jesus comes to meet His own,
  As at His feet we sing and pray;
We have a Bethel all our own,
  An altar in green Idlewood,
Our trysting place, our innermost,
  Built "In His Name" to Christ our Lord.

Dear Lakeview, home of trust and love,
  What pure and noble souls we find;
The Lord has many children here,
  With great, warm hearts like gold refined.
But some come closer, nearer drawn,
  Nestle into our hearts to stay;
We keep their memory as we go,
  To be a part of life alway.

O Flossie, with your artist soul,
  Carrie, with loving heart and true,
Dora, with presence full of joy,
  And Phebe, with her song for you,
Like fragrant breath of summer morn,
  Like dew impearled on emerald lea,
Into my life your lives have come,
  Sweet incense is your love for me.

What matter though your Phebe sits
  Nearest the treetop while she sings?
"Look up, not down," to hear her song,
  And catch the gold dust from her wings;

"Look up, not down," to see your star,
    And follow **where** she leads the way
To glorious heights yet unattained,
    Bathed in the light of heavenly day.

It matters not though **she may stand**
    Upon life's upper golden **stair;**
She reaches down her hand of **love**
    To clasp your own, to lead you higher.
So four young hearts in love are one,
    In His dear Name our offerings bring,
And from this blessed place we go,
    To better serve and **love our King.**

Dear Flossie, with your winsome ways,
    Carrie, with heart of love so true,
Dora, with sunlight in **her face,**
    Phebe, the woodbird, sings for you.
List to your songter's love refrain:
    "Phebe! Phebe!" from hilltop spire,
"Press on to reach the things before!"
    "Phebe! **Phebe!**" she calls you higher.

1887.

A Blessed Summer Sabbath at Lakeview.

A LOVING MEMORY.
Dedicated to PROF. WILLIAM F. GIBSON.

Over the polar chill of Winter,
    There comes a ray of warm pure light,
    With gold of sunshine glory, bright.

The memory of a hallowed Sabbath
  In the green grove at loved Lakeview,
  Under the arching dome of blue.

I list again the silvery echo
  Of Lakeview's mellow distant chime,
  Mingling with bells of Christmas time.

The world shut out, the Father's Presence
  Brooding upon us from above,
  Filling our hearts with peace and love.

We gather in the forest temple,
  Our souls respond to sacred song,
  As music rolls its tide along.

The voice of prayer brings Heaven nearer,
  Precious the message of the Lord,
  Borne to our hearts from spoken word.

Within our souls the heavenly kingdom,
  Jesus has come to claim His own,
  The life eternal has begun.

As through an open door to Heaven,
  We gaze where God's sweet sunshine falls,
  Gold light through leafy forest walls.

The pulsing air with praise is vibrant,
  We feel a wondrous presence near,
  God's angels surely with us here.

So sweet the hour of Vesper Service,
  It seems as if the peace of Heaven,
  Shone o'er the hallowed Sabbath even.

In charmed shades, in Idlewood,
  We linger on Enchanted Ground,
  With twilight shadows deepening round.

Joyful I sing this song of memory,
  The rhythmic sweet of summer time,
  To mingle with the Christmas chime

The pictures from that summer Sabbath
  With this glad Christmas-tide I blend
  In my heartsong for you, dear friend.

Ever with this rare day, thrice hallowed,
  Glad thoughts of you will come again,
  " For Love of Christ," and " In His Name."

The dear Lord's Day and Christmas mingle,
  Meeting as one in holy time,
  And sweeter still the joyful chime.

The music borne through leafy arches
  Is vibrant in the Christmas air,
  With holy thoughts of praise and prayer.

Your presence on this day is with me,
  Though parted, still by faith we meet
  Around the blessed Mercy Seat.

At vesper hour I feel you nearer,
  Bowing before the Father's throne
  I pray Him make you all His own.

I breathe for you a benediction,
  Upon this Sabbath Christmas day,
  God's peace abide with you alway.

Vesper hour, Dec. 4, 1892.

C. L. S. C. Vigil, Class '94.

"CULTURE, LOVE, SERVICE, CHRIST."

Night's curtain closely drawn around
  Our hallowed place, the Lakeview Grove,
The Sabbath with its blessings rare
  Has one last treasure yet of love,
                    The Vigil.

With voices hushed we climb the hill,
  And gather in the hallowed Hall ;
We listen, while from lips we love,
  The gracious words of wisdom fall
                    At Vigil Hour.

A charm these mystic letters keep
  For all who in the Circle stand,
And loyal keep in step and time
  With dear Chautauqua's glorious band,
                    C. L. S. C.

Each letter has a magic power,
  A lesson of its own to teach,
A hidden treasure to impart,
  A truth that all who seek may reach,
                    C. L. S. C.

To make the most of all we have,
  In our earth day of toil and strife,
Enlarge our gifts, our talents use,
  Enrich and broaden all the life.
                    Culture.

A loving heart can always give,
　Scatter its treasured wealth around,
And like the sun that lights the world,
　No poorer ever shall be found.

Love.

In ministry for others' good,
　Not for the sake of self alone,
Making of life a line of light,
　By deeds of loving kindness shown.

Service.

Where'er we find the Master's work,
　In willing service, high or low,
If done for Him with heart of love,
　His blessed peace shall with us go.

Christ.

Suggested by words of Dr. Hurlbut, spoken at vigil.

Munroe Cottage.

This poem is inspired by and dedicated to Miss SUSAN M. STEVENS
—"A Woman with a Faculty."

　　" How beautiful is this house. The atmosphere
　　Breathes rest and comfort, and the many chambers
　　Seem full of welcomes."—*Longfellow.*
　　　" Dux femina facti."—*Virgil.*

In shady grove at Lakeview
　Rises a new-made home,
With welcome for the stranger,
　A cordial " Hither come."

Munroe—the name is honored—
  Physician the beloved,
Whose skill in healing virtue
  So many lives have proved.

Upon a sloping hillside,
  With goodly **view it stands,**
Where daily eager learners
  Pass up in thronging bands.

A great, warm heart hath builded
  This home so sweet and fair,
With many a thought of comfort
  For weary ones to **share.**

Beneath the waving tree-tops,
  Beneath the cool green shade,
Close to the Hall **of Prayer,**
  The sweet home nest is made.

The bells in mellow chiming
  Herald the rosy dawn;
Anon sweet songs of Zion
  Float on the air of morn.

The night with dews of blessing,
  With noiseless footfall comes,
And drops her soft, dark curtain
  Over the peaceful homes.

And when the grove is gleaming
  Like lovely fairy bower,
Our cottage hangs its signals
  To grace the evening hour.

Here comes God's blessed angel
With balmy, restful sleep,
And wraps the weary toiler
In peaceful slumber deep.

A safe, sweet place of **resting**,
With hearts of Christian **love**,
Angelic guards encamping
Around the silent grove.

Within this home what comfort,
What **resting place we find,**
Here loving **care is watchful,**
Here **every heart is kind.**

Our room — a chosen home nest —
Looks toward **the rising sun,**
Chamber of Peace we find **it**
When the full day **is done.**

This cottage stands in beauty
Upon the sloping hill,
And myriad footsteps pass it,
Onward and upward still.

The summer of 1886.

To Dr. Jesse L. Hurlbut.

"The spirit of Elijah doth rest on Elisha."
"Aaron's rod was budded and brought forth buds, and bloomed
blossoms and yielded almonds."

When to our hearts the call was borne
  For the beloved John,
To take him from our head away,
  To wear a bishop's crown,
A cloud came o'er the sky of blue,
  Our sun was in eclipse,
We missed his presence, golden words
  That fell from loving lips;
When lo, the dark cloud rent in twain,
  The shadows fled away,
A pure, sweet light shone o'er the night,
  Herald of golden day.

His mantle falls, his spirit rests
  On answering spirit grand,
A chosen vessel for the work,
  The noblest of our band.
Like Aaron's almond rod preserved
  Within the holy place,
Our Rod of Jesse buds and blooms
  With flowers of truth and grace.
On holy mount he learns of God
  The pattern he has given,
And brings to us His own sure word
  To show the way to heaven.

No longer on the willow boughs
　　Our silent harps are hung,
But, tuned again to major strains,
　　Our new glad song is sung.
Thou art to us the central **light**
　　Of our Chautauqua home,
The magnet drawing loving **hearts**,
　　As to this shrine we come.
May many years of work be thine
　　To labor for the Lord,
To win at last, in His own time,
　　The Master's dear reward.

A Post-Graduate Poem.

" **Look Up**, not down.
　Look Out, not in,
　Look Forward, not back,
　Lend a Hand."
" We study the word and works of God."
" Let us keep our Heavenly Father in our midst."
" Never be discouraged."

CLASS MOTTO, '85.
" Press on, reaching after those things which are **before.**"

Again a distant echo falls on the listening ear,
The bells! the bells of Lakeview **ring out** their peals of
　　cheer.
The triune voices calling, in mellow chiming clear,
"Haste to the **grove** at Lakeview! the days we love are
　　here!"

Lakeview ! **our** hearts are thrilling at the familiar sound,
And to thy welcome summons respond with joyous bound.
The silver tones awaken the echoes far and near,
And sound with voice of gladness the welcome for us here

The fair grove smiles in beauty amid the wealth of green,
The dome of heavenly azure arching the peaceful **scene ;**
Amid the summer glory, with loyal hearts we come
Unto our spirit's Mecca, unto a rest and home.
Hail to this grove of beauty, home of the heart and mind !
Within its bowers enchanted a resting place we find,
We come with eager longing to drink from crystal springs,
We seek the **living waters that heavenly** wisdom brings.

We read in classic story **of academic grove,**
Where Plato left **his glory in life of truth and love,**
And like that charmed **story in far off days of old,**
Where lofty thoughts **of wisdom amid the trees were told,**
In this fair grove, our Lakeview, we sit at **Wisdom's** feet
And listen to her teachings all eloquent and sweet ;
On golden fruits of wisdom from trees of knowledge fair,
In these **calm shades we're feasting, with** lavish freedom
    share.

     An impulse to the work of life
       Unto our souls is daily given,
    To make each day reflect the light,
      The glory of the coming heaven.
    Upon our hearts we grave the words
      Our glorious leaders speak in love,
    Mottoes to guide us in the way
      That leads **to peace and joy above.**

"Look up!" Behold the morning skies
  Are all ablaze with amber light,
"Not down," where still the shadows drape
  The earthly vales in misty night.
"Look up!" Behold the Orient beams
  Hang out their rosy banners bright;
It comes! The banners are unfurled,
  A sunrise o'er the mountain height.

"Not down" to delve 'mid earthly dross,
  For treasure passing soon away,
"Look up!" Behold the crown of life,
  The faithful win at close of day.
"We build the rounds by which we climb"
  To shining heights on heights above,
We rise by strength we strive to gain,
  We grow by adding love to love.

Not down into the silent earth,
  Where the beloved form was laid,
"Look up!" Behold a vision fair,
  The spirit pure in light arrayed.
"Look out," with watchful, waiting eye,
  O'er earth's broad, waving, whitening field,
"Not in;" no selfish seeking soul
  Shall golden sheaves of harvest yield.

"Forward!" unto life's conflict brave,
  With glowing heart and willing hand,
No backward look, still onward press,
  To reach the glorious Promised Land.

Seek still to " lend " the helping " **hand**,"
  With every new, fresh gift of day,
To ease some over-burdened soul,
  To cheer some lonely, tearful way.

Close following in our Great Heart's steps
  The shining way of growing light,
Leading still up beyond the stars,
  Height rising still o'er distant height.
How vast the unattained that waits
  Beyond our view in vision clear,
The wondrous life that shall reveal
  What seems **so far,** yet lies so near !

Study with love the glorious word
  Of life our Father has revealed,
And find **within the** Holy Book
  Exhaustless **treasures are** concealed,
And with this matchless Book unite
  The woudrous works His hand **hath** wrought,
Lessons of wisdom, love and power,
  In all this lovely earth are taught.
We learn to trust and labor on,
  Content to do the Master's will.
Not to lose heart, fresh courage take,
  To trust 'mid clouds and darkness still.

In solitude of forest dim,
  The wood thrush pours its liquid song
For those who through the summer day
  In outside sunshine pass along.

So poet singers pour their verse
 From out a quiet resting place,
To soothe and help lone toilers brave,
 With trustful words of cheer and peace.

Such lessons blessed Lakeview gives
 To those who seek her summer shade,
Teachings that bring us nearer God,
 And life is stronger, brighter made.

Sweet comes the Sabbath stillness, a soothing, heavenly
 peace
Steals o'er the watching spirit a sense of blissful rest;
We feast on heavenly manna, we quaff the heavenly wine,
We hear sweet songs of Zion, "in notes almost divine."
From crystal fount upspringing, salvation's well so free,
With joy we draw the waters through all the blessed day.

A dream of heaven the fair grove seems,
 Where God comes down to fill the place,
With benediction full of love,
 A smile of everlasting peace;
Within that blessed heaven,
 That knows no sin, no night,
His ransomed servants serve Him,
 With tireless, pure delight.

Life at Lakeview, hallowed, peaceful,
 Like a glimpse of life above,
Where there broods o'er longing spirits
 Presence of exceeding love,

When the morning skies are lighted
  With the rosy tints of day,
Incense sweet ascends to heaven,
  As warm hearts united pray.

As within the spiral chambers
  Of the pearly ocean shell,
Music from its distant sea home,
  Low, sweet murmurs ever dwell,
So the holy vesper service,
  With its soothing, restful calm,
Lingers like the moan of sea shell,
  With a mystic, peaceful charm.

Classmates, we meet with growing love,
  And eager clasp the friendly hand,
Firm in life's highest, holiest aim,
  Shoulder to shoulder here we stand.
Still toiling on with tireless zeal,
  More priceless treasures seek to gain,
Seal after seal, through lengthening years,
  New stars for our diplomas win.

Classmates, see! there lie before us
  Heights on heights yet unattained;
Pause not in the onward marching
  Till the crown of life be gained;

    And as our poet sister sung,
    Melodious verse with silver tongue:
  "Within the soul's bright wonderland,
    We there shall know and understand,
    And all the endless ages through
    Have only angels' work to do."

July 10. 1886.

4

Sonnet.

SABBATH VESPER HOUR.

It is the hush of Sabbath vesper hour;
  It comes with holy peace and restful calm,
  With thoughts all tender as a hallowed psalm,
Resting upon my heart with holy power,
While memory brings her sweet and sacred dower,
  And breathes around my soul a soothing charm,
  Distilling **influence like a healing balm**,
With incense like sweet breath of April flower;
Thoughts of dear friends and hours **in templed grove**,
  The vesper service with its music sweet,
  I list again with longing heart and ear,
Sit **by their side in** hallowed **place we** love,
  While voices tender, words of life repeat,
  So peaceful **all, we feel our Lord is** near.

Ten Years.

1885.   July 23.   1895.

FOR THE BELOVED CLASS OF '85.

" Press on, reaching after the things that are before."

We stand upon a mount of life
  In this glad summer time,
While memory bells all joyous ring
  Their sweet-toned silver chime.

We gathered here — the 85's —
  Passed through the golden gate,
'Neath arches green o'er flower-strewed way,
  Where crowning laurels wait
        Ten years ago.

The earth took on a wondrous charm,
  The sky a deeper blue,
We felt within our souls the truth,
  " I make all things anew."
A larger life is ours to-day,
  More glorious hopes we share
Than filled our hearts as here we stood
  The graduate's crown to wear
        Ten years ago.

A backward look to see the path
  Leading through circling years,
Our joyful steps have onward come,
  And bright the way appears.
A broad horizon circles round
  This height on which we stand,
A goodly prospect lies before,
  Nearer the Promised Land
        Than ten years ago.

Within Chautauqua's borders we found the fount of youth,
Her clear, unfailing waters sparkle with light of truth.
All wondrous is the vision our eyes behold to-day,
'Tis glorious to be living to tread the King's highway.
The pulsing air is vibrant with inspiration rife,
We feel the holy impulse, the more abundant life.

The Lord of Life has risen, His glory fills the earth,
The world's bright Easter morning now shows His glory
     forth.
With light the heavens are flooded, new worlds of thought
     are found,
Wide open doors of knowledge o'er all the earth abound.
Behold the Orient glowing, the King of Day comes forth,
The sunrise gold is flooding the newly wakened earth.

It shines upon broad prairies, gilds lofty mountain height,
The Orient is radiant, Pacific shores are bright.
One hand of love has opened full many a long-closed door;
And left his shining footprints where he has trod before.
The nations are awaking, the Spirit is abroad,
O'er all dark places brooding comes the sweet light of
     God;
Oh, wondrous the awaking where night has lingered long,
Isles of the sea are listening to catch the morning song.

Nearing the century's summit, we mount from height to
     height,
Facing its open vision, its full electric light;
We hail with joy the coming, we, children of the King.
We go to meet the morning, our hearts glad anthems sing;
Onward, still onward pressing, with ever upward trend,
Till dawns the morn of glory, whose day shall have no
     end.

Our leader loved is guiding Chautauqua's triumph car,
Freighted with life and blessing to nations from afar;
He has unsealed pure fountains, opened the gates of day,
Where waters sweet are flowing, and diamond sparkles
     play.

We see the palm trees waving along the King's highway,
We join in glad hosannas, we hail the glorious day;
A chorus grand is sounding from mount and vale and sea,
The whole glad earth rejoices in one vast jubilee.

While come the days with radiant dawn,
   And part with evening's tender light,
While sweet flowers bloom and wild birds sing,
   While winds sport 'mid the cloud beds bright,
While mountains rise sublime and still,
   While sings the sea its monotone,
While Hope, Faith, Love their lessons teach,
   List to our watchword, still " Press on ; "
   " Press on to reach the things before."

On living tablets of the heart
   Our Decade's love is deeply graven,
Thrilled with the influence of this place
   We rise to meet our coming heaven.
A well of water springing up
   To everlasting life we found,
Our Lord the fountain opened wide,
   And lavish poured the crystal round.

We bring our Decade's garnered love
   To dear Chautauqua's hallowed shrine,
With glad thanksgiving to the hand
   Uplifting us to heights divine
Transfiguration of our lives,
   By holy influence breathed from heaven,
The pure, sweet thoughts from Jesus learned,
   In this grand work so freely given.

Beloved, from my heart of hearts,
  Most holy place within my soul,
I sing this memory song for you,
  Our Decade's years of love unroll.
" Invincible " we stand to-day,
  With steadfast purpose, holy aim,
To follow where our Master leads,
  Press on to conquer " In His Name."

True to our watchword, " Onward press,"
  " To reach the things that are before,"
More life, more light, more work to do,
  Till all the earthly way is o'er;
From glory unto glory still,
  From height attained to height still higher,
Until each full, symmetric life
  Is crowned with glory of the spire.

Read at the tenth anniversary of Class of '85, at Hall on the Hill,
Aug. 1, 1895.

Class Song, '85.

Gathering in our woodland temple,
  ' Neath the summer's golden rays,
From the hearts in love united,
  Comes a song of joy and praise;
Bringing here our glad oblation,
  Grateful for the wealth of thought,
And the ministry of blessing
  For our sakes so freely wrought.

On this day we, loving classmates,
  Look with grateful joy above,
For the years of work completed,
  For their fruit of peace and love.
May the precious truths we treasure
  From our Father's Holy Word,
Cause our lives to bear the image
  Of our Saviour, Christ, the Lord.

Hallowed hours we know together,
  Hours when heaven seems very near,
When we feel a sacred Presence,
  Feel our loving Lord is here.
May the pure and peaceful spirit
  Of our Master fill the place,
Brooding o'er our woodland Bethel
  With His benison of peace.

Nearer, dearer our communion
  In the hour of love and prayer,
Bringing hearts in closer union
  As its peaceful joys we share.
Press we on with earnest spirit
  For the unseen things before,
In the footsteps of the Master,
  Where He shows the open door.

Sung at Class Anniversary, Aug. 1, 1895.

Go Forward.

———

FOR THE GUILD OF SEVEN SEALS.

———

With every step we take we higher rise,
  The slope is upward whither lies our way,
The line of vision a new level strikes
  As pace by pace we mount each new-born day.

On everything the dew of morning hangs,
  Each breath we draw with sweetest fragrance rife,
The thrill of inspiration fills our souls,
  With bounding pulse of new upspringing life.

Heart answers heart, and soul to soul responds,
  As we keep step with joyful, upward trend,
Our eyes are fixed on sunlit mountain tops
  Of inspiration which enchantment lend.

A summit gained, a smooth, green table land,
  Which this glad day our feet with joy have trod,
Grand reaches still before with sunset gold,
  Beyond the sunset are the hills of God.

O'er them the everlasting morn shall rise,
  The gates will open, we shall enter in,
To the dear presence of our Master, Lord,
  To grow in love with Him we loved unseen.

1894.

A Blessed Anniversary.

1886.   Ten years at Munroe Cottage.   1896.

INSCRIBED **TO OUR PATRON SAINT,**

MISS SUSAN M. STEVENS,

" Whose many virtues charm the soul,
And whose viands cheer the body."

" How far that little candle throws its beams !
So shines a good deed in a naughty world."
— *Merchant of Venice.*

"About midway to the top of the Hill was a pleasant Arbor made
by the Lord of the Hill, for the refreshment of weary travellers."
—*Pilgrim's Progress.*

The little modest Phebe, a bird of low degree,
Here brings her loving offering, her one refrain to thee,
And sings of Munroe Cottage, with all the kindness shown
For ten love-lighted summers, that like bright dreams
      have flown.

Of all the fair homes nestling amid **our** Lakeview grove,
Munroe for us is fairest, and keeps our warmest love.
A great, **warm heart has** builded this cottage neat and fair,
That true Chautauqua pilgrims may in its comforts share.
Ten years of love and blessing this charmed home hath
      stood,
And garnered sweetest memories within our Lakeview
      wood.

So rare for situation, it gives us pleasure still,
Midway 'twixt Auditorium and Hall upon the Hill,
We rest beneath the shadow that guards us night **and day,**
Of Dr. Hurlbut's presence, **and** cannot go astray;
For like protecting angel, **encamping** close around,
Doth seem our **Lord's dear servant upon this hallowed**
    ground.

Here welcome ever waiteth, and many an honored guest,
Within **the** chambers peaceful, has sought and found
    sweet rest;
And tender thoughts awaken **of** friends we see no more,
Whose presence ne'er shall enter through the still open
    door.
They live in precious memory, safe shrined within the
    heart,
With Lakeview still their presence seems hallowed, cher-
    ished, part.

How far that little candle has shed its cheery rays!
Bright and still brighter glowing through the full decade's
    days.
Here weary workers **as they toil to Hall upon the Hill,**
May pause to rest beside the way, refresh their spirits still.

Yet more and more **we love thee, our Lakeview, hallowed,**
    dear,
Still more sweet home **ties bind us** to our heart centre here;
New beauty clothes the summer 'neath these warm amber
    skies,
With wealth **of deepest** verdure and flowers of myriad
    dyes.

We see fair morning open the golden gates of day,
The hilltops catch the sunlight upon their summits grey.
We gaze with raptured vision, when the bright day is done,
On "trailing clouds of glory" around the setting sun.

The daylight fades, and gently falls the soft twilight mist,
Veiling the distant hilltops with floating amethyst.
All silent comes the nightfall, while in the azure deep
The glorious constellations their tread majestic keep.
Amid the tender gloaming we sit in grateful thought,
To ponder well the lessons the blessed day hath brought.
Such precious friends we gather for our life-treasures here,
Such great, warm hearts we're finding, the Lord's own
    children dear.

We gather up the fragments of joy upon our way,
And keep in closer heart clasp the friends we greet to-day;
And for these days of blessing, their wealth of thought
    and love,
A joy to us forever their memory shall prove.
The night with dews of blessing with noiseless footfall
    comes,
And drops its soft, dark curtain over the Cottage homes;
Anon the Grove is gleaming like shining fairy bower,
And myriad lights make lovely the dewy evening hour.
Then with the golden morning sound the sweet bells for
    prayer,
To Normal Hall we hasten, the hallowed hour to share.

And so we count our mercies, content we gladly stay,
In this great age so restless we wander not away;
Near by the head of Lakeview, its lovely pillared crown,
By its great heart we gather, a little farther down.

Among the greater lights that shine within this classic
    Grove,
Whom we delight to honor, praise, and give our heart's
    true love,
Are the grand names that we unite on this glad day to
    sing—
Stevens, the founder of this Home—Hurlbut, our Lake-
    view king.
One hand of love has opened for us this Cottage Home,
With greeting never failing, the yearly " Hither come."

Her large, rich heart can always give, scatter its wealth
    around,
And like the sun that lights the world, no poorer e'er is
    found ;
The central light of love and joy, the angel of our hearth,
Whose presence makes this calm retreat a sweet, green
    spot of earth,
Is she whose great, warm, generous soul with love has
    filled our days ;
The grace of Christian womanhood in all her queenly ways ;
May all the kindness shown, the sunshine she has shed,
Return, increased a thousand fold, upon her blessed head.

Just an interlude of prose at this point, to bring in a
quotation from Virgil and give added dignity to this occa-
sion. What the pious Æneas said to Queen Dido, we say
to our Queen of Munroe Cottage :

" *In freta dum fluvii current, dum montibus umbrae,*
Lustrabunt convexa, polus dum sidera pascet ;
Semper honos, nomenque tuum, laudesque manebunt."

Which being interpreted means:

"While rivers shall run into the seas,
 While clouds move around the tops of the mountains,
 While heaven shall sustain the stars,
 Always thy honor and name and praise shall continue."

Long live our Saint, to keep for us
   This dear Chautauqua Home,
And all who share its hallowed joys
   At last to heaven come;
And now, for dear Miss Stevens
   Let the "white lilies" bloom,
And shed o'er Doctor Hurl'ut
   The choicest of perfume.

LAKEVIEW, July 27, 1896.

Luman Thompson Jefts.

A VOICE FROM THE CLASS OF '85.

Entered the life immortal July 3, 1896.
"Lord, I am Thine and Thou art mine." — *His dying words.*

"All hearts grew warmer in the presence
 Of one who, seeking not his own,
Gave freely for the love of giving,
 Nor reaped for self the harvest sown."
                    —*John G. Whittier.*

Dear Lord, we upward turn our spirits
   To seek Thy face in this still hour,
To music set this sacred service,
   A triumph song o'er Death's dark power.

O classmate, brother, friend beloved,
  The noblest spirit of our band,
Thy earth work done, a higher calling,
  Crowned by the loving Father's hand.

O Lakeview, 'mid thy **bowers of beauty,**
  There is a moaning like the sea,
An empty space, a vanished face,
  Where thy loved presence used to be.

O days of Lakeview life so blessed,
  From hand of love divinely given,
Like sunrise gold still brighter glowing
  Your radiance with the hues of heaven!

Thy presence seems around us lingering,
  Amid these scenes so sweet and fair,
Filled with thy life and earnest purpose,
  Thy cheerful spirit, love and **prayer.**

Still upward, round by round, his life-work,
  Waiting to hear the Master's word,
Till on the shining, **golden stairway**
  He met **the angel of the Lord.**

Like the fair stream, pure, silent, flowing,
  Marking its path with living green,
Was the true life whose love and service
  Shall still in lives he served be seen.

His living monument is builded,
  We look around us and behold
Where he has wrought his work so noble,
  More lasting than in lines of **gold.**

As light upon the clouds reflected
　Of evening, tells that lands unseen
Lie fair beyond our earth horizon
　'Neath sunrise gold in living green,

So the clear sunset of a lifetime,
　Like his all full of **holy love,**
Speaks of the pure, eternal splendor,
　Hidden from earth-veiled eyes above.

All consecrated to the Master,
　The talents, wealth to him God-given,
Scattering with lavish **hand his riches,**
　Laying his treasure safe in **heaven.**

O classmate, friend, with tender grieving,
　We sing our farewell song for thee,
And sorrow most of all that never,
　Ah, nevermore, thy face we see.

No more on **earth, but O, in heaven,**
　The Evermore shall joyful sing,
For evermore the chorus sounding
　In the glad presence of our King.

Thou'lt keep for us a loving welcome,
　As one by one we follow home,
O may it be with full lives laden,
　And glad "well done" we all **may come.**

Here as **we stand at death's dark portal,**
　We still a song of triumph raise,
That thou hast entered life immortal,
　To join God's host in heavenly praise.

We drop upon thy new-made grave-rest
This immortelle of Lakeview love,
Thy memory green we sacred cherish
Until we meet with joy above.

July, 1896.

Raindrops.

Written by request of Prof. CHARLES E. BOYD. He wrote the first
stanza and set the hymn to music.

" Welcome little raindrops,
Sing a song to me,
Patter on the window,
Patter, patter free.
Sing of thirsty flowers,
Sing of leaves and grass,
We all hear your footsteps
Pattering on the glass."

Through the evening shadows
On the roof you come,
As we snugly gather
Round the hearth of home.
Mingling with the music,
With glad hearts we raise
For the joy and love-light
Of these summer days.

Like an angel presence
  Coming from above,
Is the shower of blessing
  From the Father's love.
Causing flowers of gladness
  In life's path to bloom,
Cheering on the weary,
  With their choice perfume.

Coming still to brighten
  All the earth below,
In your fairy footsteps
  Lovely things will grow.
Lone and desert places
  Blossom like the rose,
Arched with rainbow beauty,
  Where the raindrop goes.

Sept. 8, 1896.

Welcome Home.

TO DR. JESSE L. HURLBUT.

Lift up, lift up with gladness
  Your heads, O gates of green,
As 'neath your arches passing
  The presence loved is seen.
Ye bells, ye bells of Lakeview,
  Ring out with silver voice,
Echo our deep soul gladness,
  Sound our refrain—Rejoice!

Wave your bright heads, ye treetops,
  Birds in your branches sing,
Ye winds, on harps Æolian,
  Touch every tuneful string;
Let our grand forest temple
  With glad thanksgiving ring!

Fair Lakeview for his coming
  Wears robes of freshest green,
And sunrise gold is lighting
  The waves with crystal sheen;
While throbbing hearts are hasting
  Their incense pure to bring,
And for his safe returning
  A joyful anthem sing;
With flowers we strew his pathway,
  With loving words we greet,
From out our deep soul gladness,
  For his returning meet.

A psalm of triumph singing,
  That God to us has given
Such love from His own fountain,
  To lead the way to heaven;
To show the Father's glory
  In life so good and sweet,
Doing the Master's service,
  Learning at Jesus' feet.
And so, our noble Leader,
  We come, a thronging band,
Following thy guiding footsteps
  To our Immanuel's Land.

The Lord hath been before thee,
    Leading in unseen way,
The bright Shekinah guiding
    His servant night and day,
Laden with precious spices
    From Orient lands afar,
Coming to scatter blessings
    Where thy life treasures are;
From out the Land so hallowed,
    Thy steps have gladly trod,
Thou comest in the spirit
    Of Christ, our loving Lord.

Rich dost thou come with treasure,
    To give with liberal hand
In showers of love and blessing,
    To homes throughout our land.
Thy foot hath scaled the mountain,
    In grand cathedral trod,
In hallowed places lingered,
    Where walked the Son of God.
The Lord of Life has risen,
    His glory fills the earth,
The world's bright Easter morning
    Now shows His glory forth.

The Lord hath been thy Keeper,
    Thy Guide through changing way,
Preserving thy outgoing,
    Thy coming, day by day.
And so we come with gladness
    To this memorial feast,

A heart-warm welcome bringing,
Our loved and **honored guest.**
A sacramental season,
Our banquet hour is given,
Love's banner o'er us waving,
Foretaste of joy in heaven.

1897.

---

ffloreber.

FOR LAKEVIEW ASSEMBLY

The Daily had reported that the Assembly was to come to Framingham for five years.

"For five years!" said Dr. Vincent. "This is a mistake. It is to come for fifty years; yes, and forever."—*Assembly of 1884.*

> "Men may come and men may go,
>   But I go on forever."
>   —*Tennyson.*

Somewhat back from the Framingham street
Is a lovely grove, a green retreat;
Beyond the guarded **portico**
Tall, waving trees their shadows throw,
And from their place near **Normal Hall**
The triune bells of Lakeview **call**
                  Forever—ever!
                  Ever—forever!

And here within this classic grove
Our lives are like a dream of love;
Soul answers soul, while we are fed
From royal feast so lavish spread;
Rich freighted days of sunrise gold
The dear Assembly seasons hold,
     Forever—ever!
     Ever—forever!

Here comes the hour of morning prayer,
And songs of praise are in the air;
The "Chorus" with grand symphony
Fills all the grove with melody;
The days are full of work and joy—
Mind, heart and soul find blest employ,
     Forever—ever!
     Ever—forever!

From lips all eloquent are given
Teachings that lift the soul to heaven;
Treasures by gifted minds are brought,
To broaden life, enrich our thought,
And Sabbath hours with peace and calm
Fill all the place with hallowed charm,
     Forever—ever!
     Ever—forever!

Here groups of happy children play,
In Idlewood fond lovers stray;
O precious hours! O golden prime!
The affluence of assembly time!

Our loyal hearts count up the gold,
The treasures rare we sacred hold,
> Forever — ever !
> Ever — forever !

From pillared Hall upon the Hill
The graduates come, fresh ranks to fill,
Through golden gate, neath flower-wreathed arch,
With waving banners join the march,
A goodly host — C. L. S. C. —
And greater glory yet to be,
> Forever — ever !
> Ever — forever !

Here is a fountain opened wide,
That flows a pure and living tide,
And here the longing soul may take
The crystal clear its thirst to slake,
May know on earth the joy of heaven,
The foretaste now so freely given,
> Forever — ever !
> Ever — forever !

And here this heaven-sent work has come,
To make itself a lasting home,
The Assembly's here — has come to stay —
Its place prepared — Lakeview — alway !
The bells their peal of joy shall ring,
Glad pæans from our hearts we sing,
> Forever — ever ! .
> Ever — forever !

Here crowds may come and crowds may go,
But, like the river's ceaseless flow,
The Assembly ever shall go on
Until its blessed work is done.
Go on and prosper, good and great,
A glory to our honored State;
God guide and keep forever, aye,
Till all of earth has passed away!

            Forever — ever!
            Ever — forever!

Sept. 23, 1896.